Please return/renew this item
by the last date shown.
Books may also be renewed by
phone and Internet

Published in 2007 in Great Britain by
Barrington Stoke Ltd
18 Walker Street, Edinburgh EH3 7LP

www.barringtonstoke.co.uk

ISBN: 978-1-84299-477-1

Printed in Great Britain by Bell & Bain Ltd

A Note from the Author

When you lose someone close to you, they do not go away – not all at once. They can still surprise you. You find one of their hairs on the collar of your coat. In an old plastic bag you see a shopping list in their writing. You flip open your phone, and some of the messages they sent you are still there – and you just can't bear to delete them.

That's normal. It happens to everyone. But what happens when the person you have lost wants you to follow them?

That's where *Kiss of Death* comes in ...

This one's for Charlotte

Contents

Chapter 1
Kate

Nick looked out of the bus window. He was fed up. It was raining, but that wasn't the problem.

When Kate got onto the bus, she sat next to Nick as she always did.

"Budge up!" she said.

Nick looked round at her as she sat down, but he didn't say "Hello". He only grunted, and drew stickmen on the misty window glass.

"What's the matter with you, today?" Kate asked as the bus swung into the High Street. "You haven't said a word."

"Nothing to say." Nick's nose was still pressed flat against the window, but he

wasn't looking at the street. His eyes were half shut.

"Don't be so boring! I think I'll go and sit next to someone else," said Kate.

"No, don't." Nick looked at her. Kate was small, with dark hair and glossy red lips. She had a funny way of wrinkling up her nose when she smiled. She smiled a lot at Nick. In fact, she was smiling now. Her friends said she was in love with him, but Nick knew better. They were friends, that was all. Friends who liked to have a bit of fun.

"My weekend's a mess," said Nick. He tried to sound glum, but Kate's smile always cheered him up. "No money, no credit, and my Uncle David's coming to stay." He made a face, as if he had just taken a swig of vinegar.

"What's up with Uncle David?" asked Kate.

"He's the meanest man in Britain. If he lends you a paper hanky, he expects you to write a thank-you note."

Kate sniffed. "Sounds like a jerk."

"Mind you, he's rich. He drives a Jag."

"You know what?" said Kate. "I can tell the future. Here, just look into my eyes." She frowned, and swayed about, as if she was in a trance. "Yes, I'm right. You're going to get some money very soon."

"I bet!" grinned Nick.

"You can make fun of me," said Kate, "but I'm never wrong about things like that. You'll see! And forget about stupid Uncle David, OK?"

"I will. If he lets me."

"Poor thing," mocked Kate. "Let me kiss it better." She leaned over.

"Isn't this your stop?" asked Nick.

"Eek!"

The bus had already pulled up, and Kate still had to rush along the top deck. She grabbed her wet coat and ran. As she got to the top of the stairs she turned and shouted back to Nick. "Be happy! And don't forget, you owe me a kiss!"

"It's a promise!" Nick called back, grinning.

Kate vanished down the steps to the lower deck of the bus. Then Nick saw her

mobile phone, lying on the seat beside him. It must have fallen out of her coat pocket as she got up.

Nick stood up. Maybe there was just time to catch Kate? But no, the bus was already pulling out from the kerb, into the busy traffic. Nick shook his head and put the phone into his own pocket. He'd call Kate's landline later, to tell her it was safe.

Just then there was a scream, out in the street. A horn blasted. The bus braked hard, and Nick was flung back into his seat.

Then came a crash and a crunch of metal, and the scream suddenly stopped. Everyone on the top deck of the bus was leaning over to see was going on.

"What is it?" asked the woman behind Nick.

"That girl," said her husband. "The one who got off in such a hurry just now. She wasn't looking where she was going, and that motorbike – "

He didn't finish his sentence.

11

"What a mess," said the woman, looking down into the gutter. "She didn't stand a chance."

The road outside was dark with rain and loud with traffic. On the road Nick saw a crumpled motorbike, its wheel sticking out at a crazy angle. People were helping the rider to his feet. He did not seem badly hurt, but on the ground beside him was another person. A girl, with dark hair and bright red lips.

It was Kate. Except that now, her whole face was red.

Bloody, raw and red.

It was no longer a face at all.

Chapter 2
Easy Money

When Nick woke up the next day he felt empty. A large, dark pit had opened up in his mind. He didn't dare to look into the pit. He knew that something awful was waiting for him there. For a few seconds he could not think what it was. Then he saw

Kate's phone on his bedside table, and he remembered last night.

The ambulance. The police. All the hanging around. Waiting to give a statement.

Even at the time it had seemed like a dream.

He'd wanted to go to the hospital with Kate, but they'd said, "No". "You aren't family," the ambulance man had said. Then he had added in a different voice: "Anyway, there's nothing you can do."

The way he had said it had let Nick know for certain that Kate was dead. His friend. His best friend. Kind, funny, lively Kate – was gone. One second she had been asking him for a kiss. Then she wasn't there any more.

It was only when he'd got home that he'd found he still had her mobile phone in his pocket. The battery had been running low, and for some reason he'd plugged it in before he went to bed. Stupid – as if that would bring her back!

He got dressed. He could hear Uncle David's loud voice. They were having breakfast downstairs. When Mum had fetched Nick home last night, Uncle David hadn't said a word. He'd just sat reading a book, as if nothing had happened. Kate had been right – Uncle David was a jerk.

Nick decided not to have breakfast. He wasn't hungry anyway.

As he left his room, there was a sound behind him. He knew that tune well: Save Your Kisses For Me.

Kate's phone! Someone must have sent Kate a text. But Nick had switched the phone off last night – hadn't he? He shook his head. Last night was all a misty blur.

Unknown Caller, it said on the screen. He flipped the phone open and read the text.

Hi Nick. Don't worry about me. I'm OK – just lonely. I miss you tho. I fixed your cash problem! Kate.

Nick shivered. This was sick. Who had sent this text? Using Kate's name, too! Pretending to be her. Who would do a thing like that?

He slammed the phone back onto the table.

Only – how could they have known about his cash problem? And what had they "fixed"?

Uncle David stumbled into Nick's room just then. Nick had never seen him so pale. Most of the time, Uncle David's mouth was set in a thin, mean line. Now it was hanging open.

"I was s-sorry to hear about your friend," mumbled Uncle David. "Here – here, take this." He was holding out two £20 notes. His hand was shaking, and there was sweat on his skin. Nick saw that Uncle David kept looking behind him – as if there was someone there. "Take it!" he said. "See, I'm giving it to you!"

Uncle David thrust the notes into Nick's hand. Then he turned and ran out of the room. Nick went after him, and watched him bound down the stairs. Nick began to turn away. Then he saw the long mirror at the end of the landing.

There was someone else in the mirror apart from himself. Nick blinked. No. No, it must have been a trick of the light.

Yet, just for a second, he was sure there had been a face in the glass. A pale face, with a smile he knew very well.

Its bright red lips had been blowing him a kiss.

Chapter 3
Lonely Heart

Nick's head was spinning as he came back to his room. But he did not have time to think. The tune from Kate's phone started almost at once.

"Save your kisses for me – save all your kisses for me ..."

Nick went to grab the phone, then stopped short. This was too much. Just because someone was sending texts, that didn't mean he had to read them, did it?

But it might be important. He had to see.

Still, his hand shook a little as he opened the phone and read.

Do I get a thank you? It's lonely here, Nick. Still waiting for that kiss ... Kate.

Nick dropped the phone as if it had bitten him. It landed on the carpet at his feet. After a moment the glow of the screen faded. There was only a plastic case, with metal and wires and a clever chip inside. A mobile phone couldn't be haunted. Or could it?

He forced himself to pick it up again, slid off the back casing, then flipped out the SIM card and the battery. That should fix it.

"I must be going crazy," he thought, "to be scared of a phone."

But the memory of that face in the mirror was still with him. Either he really was going crazy, or else – or else that had been Kate.

All at once, Uncle David's terror made sense. Kate could have scared Uncle David into giving him that money, all right. If Kate was a ghost.

That was too much for Nick. He had to get out of the house – go to town – see some mates. Anything to take his mind off what was happening. He remembered the £20 notes in his pocket. He even had cash now. Plenty for the bus.

No.

He would walk after all.

He went to the bathroom to brush his teeth and wash. He was quick about it. Every time he looked in the mirror, he knew that something else was hovering in the bathroom beside him. Something solid, or not so solid, just behind him. It was human in size, with a smear of red where its mouth should be. But when he looked right at it, there was nothing to be seen.

Nick walked to town. He saw his mates, Jem, Dave and Sarah. But they wanted to talk about Kate, of course, and the way she died. He should have known there would be no escaping it. They drifted down the High Street afterwards, but that was worse. Past the shops they went, the four of them: Jem, Dave, Sarah, Nick. But reflected in every shop window he saw a fifth person walking, someone at the edge of the group – a girl. Why did no one else seem to see her?

He made for home, staying well away from the shopping streets, and keeping his eyes on the pavement in front of his feet.

"That phone of yours has been going off all day," said his mum, as he came through the front door.

"I forgot to take it with me," mumbled Nick. He thought she was talking about his own phone.

"It's been annoying your uncle. He's not himself today."

"I'm sorry."

"That's OK, love," said his mum. "But where did you get that awful ring tone? Save Your Kisses For Me? That was already naff when I was young."

Nick ran to his room, and grabbed Kate's phone. The battery and SIM card still lay beside it. The phone should be dead – should stay dead. But there were 20 unread texts waiting for him. He flipped open the lid and read again ...

Where's my kiss, Nick? I've been so lonely!

... so lonely ...

... so lonely ...

... so lonely ...

... so lonely ...

I'M SO LONELY! I WANT YOU – KATE.

Chapter 4
Kiss Chase

Late that afternoon Nick stood on the bridge over the river. The water beneath him flowed deep and dark. You could not see the bottom. He pushed Kate's phone off the railing, and heard it *plop*. The battery and SIM card followed a few seconds later. The dark river flowed on.

"Goodbye, Kate," said Nick. It felt as if he was burying her. His own private funeral. "I'll miss you," he said, "but you're gone now. I'm sorry it's got to be like this. Goodbye."

He set off back to the house, telling himself he had done the right thing, getting rid of that phone. It was better this way – for Kate, too. She wouldn't want to be stuck half-way between life and death like that, would she? Not the Kate he knew.

He felt better about it already.

Then his own phone rang in his pocket.

Unknown Caller.

"Hello?" said Nick. He heard the shake in his voice.

The caller's voice was nearly drowned by the sound of grinding engines and brakes, but he knew it at once.

"It's the girl of your dreams, Nick. I've waited too long. I'm coming for my kiss, now. Don't play hard to get ..."

There was no more, just the squeal of brakes, the roar of an engine and a motorbike horn. Even when Nick threw down the phone he could still hear them. They seemed to go on for ever.

Nick ran. He ran from the bridge and into the park, past the little kids in their sand pits and the couples walking hand in hand. He ran until he could run no longer, and had to bend over to catch his breath in the shelter of a bus stop. The light was fading, and the road was busy with rush hour traffic.

42

But what was he running from, he asked himself? A *voice*? A voice on a phone? Was that all?

He looked back down the street, and saw her.

It was Kate. She was walking towards him, coming from the park. She wasn't running, but she wasn't stopping either. He could see her bright red lips from here. No one else on the street gave any sign of having seen her.

Already she was half-way to him and
coming closer. Surely that was impossible!
She was walking the way Kate always
walked – as if she had all the time in the
world. Yet she was almost by his side.

Nick turned to run again – and suddenly
there was Kate next to him in the bus
shelter.

"Going my way?" asked Kate, wrinkling
her nose. She smiled at him. "Kiss me,
Nick. You promised."

"I – I can't," gasped Nick.

Then the smiling face changed. It didn't change all at once. First the pale skin and dark hair melted away, leaving raw, red flesh. Then Nick watched in horror as the raw flesh peeled back too. The face in front of him was nothing but snow-white bone. Kate's smile was the grinning of a skull.

She threw herself at him and he backed away – away from the shelter, away from her open arms.

"I'm so glad to have you with me, Nick!" said the death's head, in a voice like the whisper of dry grass in the wind. Her bony arms were round his neck.

"No!" cried Nick.

He didn't even hear the warning shouts from the passing shoppers, or the screech of brakes from the van behind him, as he stepped back off the pavement into the speeding traffic ...

Barrington Stoke would like to thank all its readers for commenting on the manuscript before publication and in particular:

Lewis Bean
Craig Blundell
Michael Bulmer
Gemma Coates
Jack Curtis
Jane Eastcrabbe
Nick Fan
Ashley Hilton-Dowse
Reece Holdsworth
Liz Hutton
Kellie Jackling
Ryan Loft
Joshua Mack

Mary Nolan
Alex O'Connell
Billy Pardoe
Chris Shields
Megan Simpkin
Katie Stanley
Andrew Thomson
Danny Tissington
Sue Tomlinson
Danny Underwood
Suzanne Washbrook
Kayleigh Whittaker
Chris Williams
Robbie Yearnshire

Become a Consultant!

Would you like to give us feedback on our titles before they are published? Contact us at the address below – we'd love to hear from you!

Email: info@barringtonstoke.co.uk
Website: www.barringtonstoke.co.uk

More exciting titles ...

Thing
by
Chris Powling

Black button eyes.

Zig-zag mouth.

Stiff body.

Thing.

Once it was Robbie's best friend.

Now it's become his enemy ...

**You can order *Thing* directly from our website at
www.barringtonstoke.co.uk**

More exciting titles ...

Mutant
by
Theresa Breslin

Someone is trying to steal the work in the Clone Unit.

But who is it and why are they doing it?

Anything could happen if the research gets into the wrong hands.

So who can Brad trust?

You can order *Mutant* directly from our website at www.barringtonstoke.co.uk

More exciting titles ...

Alien
by
Tony Bradman

THE WORLD AT WAR

The aliens are attacking!

Everyone must fight.

But just who is the enemy?

You can order *Alien* directly from our website at
www.barringtonstoke.co.uk

More exciting titles ...

Shark!
by
Michaela Morgan

Mark knows about sharks.

He knows how they think, live and hunt.

**He doesn't know there's a hungry shark out
there, right now.**

And it's coming his way ...

**You can order *Shark!* directly from our website at
www.barringtonstoke.co.uk**